Hanging
on to **Home**

KLASKY
CSUPO ᴵɴᶜ

Based on the TV series *The Wild Thornberrys*® created by Klasky Csupo, Inc.
as seen on Nickelodeon®

ISBN 0-439-36608-9

12 11 10 9 8 7 6 5 4 3 2 1   2 3 4 5 6 7/0

Printed in the U.S.A.

First Scholastic printing, January 2002

Hanging
on to **Home**

by Cathy East Dubowski and Mark Dubowski

SCHOLASTIC INC.

New York Toronto London Auckland Sydney
Mexico City New Delhi Hong Kong Buenos Aires

A Letter from Eliza

Hi! I'm Eliza Thornberry. I'm twelve years old and part of your average family. I have a dad, a mom, and a teenage sister named Debbie. Well, there *is* Donnie—we found him in the jungle. And Darwin the chimpanzee? He found us.

Oh, yeah, about our house. It moves! It's a big safari-van called a Commvee. It's got a table and places to sleep and just about everything we need to camp anywhere. Would you believe it travels on land and water? We really need it because we travel all over the world. You see, my dad hosts this TV nature show, and my mom films it.

Okay, so maybe we're not that average. And between you and me, something amazing happened to me. It's really cool, but totally secret. And you know what? Life's never been the same. . . .

You want to know my secret? Well . . . promise not to tell anyone? Okay, the secret is . . . I can talk to animals!

Believe me, that comes in handy when you're traveling all over the world! Like the time my family went to film orang-utans on the island of Sumatra. . . .

Chapter 1

"Land ho!" I cried.

My family's Commvee had just sailed across the Indian Ocean! I felt like an explorer on the high seas, about to discover a new world.

"Ewwww . . . ," Debbie groaned, looking a little green. She was lying on her bunk with one arm draped over her eyes, and her *Teenage Wasteland* magazine on the floor. The grungy face of her favorite rock star—Des Brodean—snarled from the cover.

"If you're feeling seasick," I told her, "it might help to go up on the roof and get some fresh air."

Anything would be better for you than lying in bed reading magazine articles about Des Brodean, I thought.

"What's making me sick is not the sea," Debbie said, scowling. "What's making me sick is going to another place far, far away from civilization! I mean, haven't we already done Sumatra?"

Sumatra is a large island that is part of the country of Indonesia, in Southeast Asia, and it's pretty remote. There are cities on the island, but it's mostly volcanoes grown over by thick jungle.

We were headed really way out, toward the north end. I mean, if we wanted a pizza, we would have had to make it ourselves—from scratch. Debbie would call that Extreme Cooking. Anything that's not takeout is pretty extreme to her. Even takeout is sort of a big deal for her; having it delivered is more her style.

The important thing to know about Sumatra is that it's just about the last place on Earth, besides the nearby island of Borneo, where orangutans still live in the wild.

That's why we went. You probably know my dad from his TV show, *Nigel Thornberry's Animal World*. My mom does all the camera and audio work for the show. They'd been invited to Sumatra by a group called the Adopt an Orangutan Society. Mom and Dad were going to shoot a documentary about the great ape known as *orang hutan,* which means "man of the forest."

Imagine. Wild orangutans! I couldn't wait to talk to them.

"Quick!" Dad suddenly shouted out. "Everyone come have a look-see!" He had one hand on the wheel. With his other hand he held up a telescope and gazed at our destination. "Smashing!"

Right away, Dad's voice says two things about him. One, he's very cheerful. Two, he's very British!

"Fasten your seat belts, everyone," my mom reminded us. She's the practical, down-to-earth one in our family.

Before we knew it—*bump!*—the Commvee's big tires touched down on the beach. Dad drove slowly on the sand. Above us were the greenest mountains I'd ever seen. Tall palm trees grew out of the sand like beach umbrellas. The sun was hot and bright, the air moist and muggy. I loved it!

"Hello, American TV-show people!" someone called. A small man walked out of the trees.

Dad waved. "We're the Thornberrys!" he shouted.

"Yes, my name is Panga. I'm with the

Adopt an Orangutan Society," the man replied as he hopped into the Commvee. "This way!" Panga said, and my dad drove where he pointed.

"Orangutans are slow-moving and can be quite easily captured," Dad told us. "Many are sold to zoos and exotic pet owners around the world. The Adopt an Orangutan Society is trying to prevent that!"

"By putting them up for adoption?" I said.

Mom smiled. "Not that kind of adoption," she said. "The 'homes' they find for the orangutans are forests. The society collects money to set up animal preserves in Sumatra where orangutans can run free."

"I hate this place," my sister, Debbie, mumbled.

Panga led us up the jungle road along the top of a rock cliff with a great view of a wide, slow-moving river. Then, all of a sudden, the forest cleared—we were at a tiny airport! There was a small runway and a plain-looking building with a sign in front that said ADOPT AN ORANGUTAN SOCIETY, SUMATRA OFFICE.

Panga noticed me looking quizzically at a small mountain of tractor tires in the yard.

"Sumatran river rafts," he explained.

"Awesome!" I said. "Can I try one?"

Panga looked at Mom. "There's one tied to a tree at the river's edge. Along with some flotation vests."

Mom nodded and said, "Okay."

"Come on, Darwin!" I said, dragging him toward the water.

"But there's no lifeguard," Darwin said as I strapped on his flotation vest. "Are-Are you sure it's safe, Eliza?"

I nodded and pulled the raft in with the anchor line.

"All aboard," I told Darwin.

Darwin's mouth fell open. "What, no deck chairs? Where are the seats? Where are the handles?"

"There aren't any," I said, laughing. "You just perch on the side and shove off!"

The trees hung over us like a huge tent as we floated along. Birds sang, insects buzzed, fish splashed. It was so peaceful.

"Wildlife alert," Darwin said, pointing toward me.

I carefully followed his finger, then ducked my head down to take a look under my seat. There, in the dark rim of the big tire, was a pair of big brown eyes staring out.

Orangutan eyes! Wow! I was nose-to-nose with a baby orangutan!

Chapter 2

It blinked as if it had just woken up from a nap. I almost laughed, but I didn't. I didn't want to scare it away.

The orangutan stared at me with big, curious, dark brown eyes—and I shivered. Its eyes looked like human eyes! For a moment, we just studied each other. Did it think we looked alike too?

Dad says great apes—that includes gorillas, orangutans, and chimpanzees (like Darwin)—are our closest relatives in the animal kingdom. Darwin likes to think that he and I may be cousins.

When I looked at this baby, I could see what Dad meant. I mean, this cute orangutan really looked like a hairy human baby!

Then I noticed the orangutan's tiny hands. They seemed like my hands, only hairier! A broad palm, four fingers, and—I giggled—it was even sucking its thumb!

This baby must be really young, I thought. Slowly, slowly, I reached out my hand. . . .

"Yeek!" the orangutan cried.

Oh, no! Before I could even say hello, the little orangutan scrambled out of the hollow shell of the tire and dove off. It didn't hit the water, though. It grabbed the dock line and climbed up, hand over hand, as if it were going up a jungle vine.

"Come back!" I called after it. "We won't hurt you!"

"Better stay on the lookout for the mother," Darwin warned, looking up into the trees. "That one was much too young to be traveling alone."

"I'd love to meet its mother!" I exclaimed.

"Not me!" Darwin replied with a shiver. "Mothers can get awfully cranky if they think someone's messing around with their precious little tots!"

"If they see me hanging out with you," I said to Darwin, "they'll figure I'm okay."

"Don't be too sure," Darwin replied. "I think orangutans come from the hermit side of the family."

I waited just the same. The minutes ticked by. I watched and I waited. But the baby orangutan never returned. And there was no sign of its mother anywhere.

"I hope the little orangutan isn't lost," I said.

"I'm sure its mother will find it," Darwin said. "Mothers always do."

I sighed. "I hope you're right." I looked across the water. The reflection of the trees made the river green. A puff of wind stirred the leaves, and Darwin flinched. I guess he was worrying about who might show up next.

"Okay, Darwin," I finally said, "we'll go find Mom and Dad." I pulled the dock line and brought us ashore. We started to climb the hill from the riverbank to the buildings. "I can't wait to tell them I spotted our first orangutan!"

We checked the Commvee and found Debbie reading *Teenage Wasteland* magazine. Her rock star idol, Des Brodean, was—as usual—brooding on the cover.

"Hey, Deb, we saw an orangutan!" I said.

Debbie gave me a bored look. "I hate this place," she said, and stuck her nose back in the magazine.

Darwin and I eventually found Mom and Dad in Panga's office, looking at a map.

"Pumpkin!" Dad said with a cheerful smile. "How was the water?"

"It was great," I replied, "especially when the orangutan showed up!"

Dad and Mom and Panga all looked surprised. "Orangutan? Here at the camp?" Panga asked. "Are you sure?"

I nodded.

Mom was already adjusting her camera lens. "Let's take a look!" she said.

"Smashing idea!" Dad said. Quickly the grown-ups followed us out the door.

"It was just a baby," I told them as we came to the river.

"Don't worry, orangutan mothers take good care of their children," Mom tried to reassure me.

Panga nodded. "They are probably far away by now." I figured he must be right.

We didn't see anything around the raft.

"I'm sure we'll see scads of orangutans tomorrow in the jungle," Dad said cheerfully.

That night after supper Panga entertained us with a local ghost story about a mountain spirit called Rabi.

"Everybody's afraid of Rabi," he said. According to the legend Rabi lives inside an old tree in the rain forest. If a logger tries to cut down this tree, Rabi appears. His long hair hangs down like vines, his face shines like the sun, and—*poof!*—Rabi turns the logger into a tree! The problem is, you never know which tree is Rabi's. That's why, Panga told us, you should never cut down an old tree.

Later I lay in bed and looked out my window at the big old trees around our camp. I wasn't thinking about Rabi, though. I was thinking about the baby orangutan.

I hoped it was all right.

Chapter 3

Pancakes. I smelled pancakes.

"Debbie, wake up!" I said. It was still dark, but I knew it must be morning. "Dad's making pancakes!"

"I still hate this place," Debbie complained as we followed the smell to the picnic table outside. There was Dad cooking on a camp stove.

"Good morning, poppets!" Dad flipped two large pancakes into the air just as a bird flew by. "Oh, my goodness!" he exclaimed. "Did you see that hornbill?

That banana-shaped beak? It's as long as the rest of the bird! Fascinating!" He whirled around to admire the bird in flight.

Unfortunately, as Dad turned to look he swung the frying pan around. Mom grabbed a plate and caught the flying pancakes seconds before they hit the dirt.

"Isn't it incredible, Marianne?" Dad gasped, his eyes still on the bird.

"Fascinating," she told Dad as she winked at me.

I grinned as I took the plate. Mom and Dad—what a team!

Debbie and I sat down. As we ate, Mom and Dad told us about the exciting day ahead of us—we would be exploring the untamed jungle of Sumatra!

"Panga has two boats waiting to carry us upriver to the jungle's interior," Dad told us. "It will be quite an adventure, poppets."

"Jungles are boring," Debbie muttered.

"I wouldn't call an untamed jungle boring," Mom said.

"That reminds me of some very useful information I picked up while we were in Borneo," Dad said. "Never get on a log that's floating against the current."

Mom frowned. "You mean, it could be a crocodile."

"Precisely!" Dad exclaimed. "Fortunately, crocs haven't yet migrated to Sumatra. But Sumatra does have tigers. You don't want to ride one of those, either."

My dad is a virtual encyclopedia of interesting information. Sometimes it's just hard to know what page he's on.

"Time to clear the table, everyone," Mom said, quickly changing the subject from crocodiles and tigers.

A few minutes later we left the air-conditioned Commvee and headed for the dock. Besides my lunch, I'd already packed a notebook and some pens in my backpack the night before. The only other thing I was carrying was a small flashlight in my pocket—you never knew when you'd need that. Debbie's pack was full of her magazines.

Mom and Dad carried the video equipment in waterproof bags, since we were traveling by boat. Darwin and Donnie followed behind.

The dock was really just a couple of tree trunks on the riverbank with a board nailed across to make a rail for tying up the boats.

"We'll split up into two groups," Dad announced while Panga got the outboard engines running in the open boats. "Marianne, Debbie, and the video equipment will go in the head boat with Panga. Eliza, Darwin, Donnie, and I will follow in the other."

We all climbed in, then waited while

Panga untied the lines. Then he dropped them into the boats and hopped into Mom's boat as the current began to pull us out slowly. When we reached the middle, Panga and Dad started the propellers in each boat and pointed them upriver.

The sun was beginning to rise as we made our way through the jungle. The water was green from the reflection of the trees that grew all the way to the water's edge. It felt like a ride up a long, green tunnel.

I turned to Darwin. "Isn't this cool?" I whispered.

Darwin fanned himself with a big leaf. "Actually, it's extremely hot," he whispered back.

I laughed. He was right. It was early in the morning and already steamy. That's the way it is in countries on the equator—all year long!

A few minutes after we left Panga's dock, the sides of the river squeezed in. The water sprayed and boats rocked up and down. Then we turned a corner, and the water was as flat and calm as a lake again.

"Keep an eye out for floating trees," Dad said. "Loggers use this river to send the trunks to the sawmills."

I stared at Dad when I finally understood what he was saying. "Cutting down orangutan houses to make people houses . . . ," I said. "No wonder they're endangered!"

"Yes, and they also have to face forest fires—and poaching."

"That's like kidnapping, isn't it?" I asked.

"You could say that. It's illegal to catch or ship a wild orangutan out of Indonesia, but that doesn't stop some people who can make a lot of money selling them as exotic pets."

Three hours later we came to a beautiful waterfall spilling off a mountain of black rocks. Panga steered us into a side creek, where we tied up the boats.

From there we followed a beaten path that Panga called an elephant walk—a trail used by elephants—to a tall banyan tree. It was Panga's landmark for the entrance to the forest where he told us we would see orangutans. We put down our camping gear, and Panga gave us our instructions. "Go in straight, fifty meters, and wait," he told us.

"Why isn't Panga coming with us?" I asked my dad as we climbed through vines and twisted tree trunks.

"It's his rather clever way to keep us from getting lost," he explained. "If we get turned around in here, we can call out, and Panga will answer back from the trail, informing us of our position."

"This looks like a good spot," Mom said, and we settled down to wait.

It was only a few minutes, but it seemed like forever until we finally heard a rustle in the leaves. Mom quietly switched on her camera. Then I saw it—a graceful red ape swinging from one tree branch to another, like a trapeze artist. Other orangutans soon followed.

"Undeniable proof," Dad whispered into a microphone, "that these animals are not the solitary creatures they are said to be. I believe that as long as there is sufficient food and habitat, orangutans will socialize with others of their kind."

Suddenly something big moved in the undergrowth! The orangutans heard it first and vanished into the treetops. Dad touched his finger to his lips—shh! What was coming? Was it poachers?

The leaves parted . . . and it was only Panga. But he had scary news.

"Time to come out," he whispered. "Tiger signs."

Debbie groaned. "I hate this place."

We quickly followed him out and cruised the boats back to camp without needing the motors. When we bumped our boats on Panga's dock at last, there was a surprise waiting for us.

"Debbie, look!" I exclaimed, not fully believing what I saw.

"What is it now?" she said, without looking up. "A purple-bellied sapsucker? An itsy-bitsy goo-goo bug? A rare, ruby-throated worm?"

I pointed at the private jet that was parked on the runway not far from our Commvee. Somebody's name was painted on the side in glittery, silver letters.

"Look, Debbie," I said. "He's here too."

Debbie slowly dragged her long blond

hair out of her eyes and stared.

"OH, MY GOSH!" she screamed as she grabbed my arm. "DES! DES BRODEAN! OH, I LOVE THIS PLACE!"

Chapter 4

"Des . . . Des . . . ," Debbie gasped. She raised a hand toward the plane the way a person lost in the desert would reach toward a mirage.

But what was Des Brodean doing here? Even Debbie couldn't think of a reason that made sense. Rock stars like Des jetted around the world to places like Paris, London, Tokyo, and L.A. But to a jungle in Sumatra? I don't think Panga's camp even had a CD player!

Just then a man rushed toward us.

He was wearing a shirt with a picture of a world map and the words DES BRODEAN UNSANITARY TOUR in big, bold letters. His stringy, sun-streaked brown hair was pulled back into a short ponytail, and he looked like he was about Mom's age.

"Marianne Thornberry?" the man exclaimed with a smile. "Is it really you?"

Being recognized in public by strangers is something that happens to my dad all the time. We've kind of gotten used to it. People know his face from the TV show. But Mom?

"Who do you think that is?" I asked Debbie. "Maybe somebody she went to high school with?"

"Yeah, right," Debbie said sarcastically. "And she just happened to run into him in the jungle?"

She was right. It didn't seem likely. And besides, Mom wasn't a Thornberry in high school.

"I'm sorry," Mom finally managed to say. "I don't think we've met."

"You're right," the man said. "I'm so sorry. I'm Free!"

"You're free?" Mom asked, puzzled.

"Scott Free's the name!" he said. "I recognized your husband from your show—and I certainly recognize you from the python episode!"

"Oh, that!" Mom blushed and shook her head. That was the one time Mom actually appeared on camera, to help hold the tail of a python.

"What I really like about the show is the camera work," Scott explained. "You see, I'm a cameraman myself!"

"Oh, my gosh!" Debbie gasped, and shoved me aside. "Are you making a Des Brodean video?"

"As a matter of fact, I am," Scott replied.

"Here?" I exclaimed. "In the middle of nowhere?"

"Panga contacted us about doing a fund-raiser for the orangutan society, and how could we say no? The little monkeys are so cute!"

"Um, they're apes," I said. "The orangutans, I mean. As opposed to monkeys."

"They're still cute!" he said.

"Mr. Free!" Debbie blurted out. "Is there any way you could get me a part in the video? Like, could I be in a crowd, and then Des picks me out, and I become his girlfriend? Wouldn't that be awesome? Don't you think I have a certain look that's right for this?"

By this point Debbie was practically clutching the front of his Unsanitary Tour T-shirt.

"Yes, well . . . uh . . . ," he stammered. "Perhaps an audition?"

"Oh, that would be just so great," Debbie said breathlessly. In her mind she was already headed for the music video awards. She tossed her hair back and gave him a Des Brodean snarl. "What would you like to see?"

Scott frowned at the ground, thinking. Then he looked up and said, "Scream."

Debbie frowned at him. "Excuse me?"

"Can you scream?"

Debbie raised one eyebrow. "I don't get it."

"Scream," Scott said again. He made a frame with his hands and looked through them, as if he were looking at her through the lens of a camera. "You know, like a fan. At a concert. Des comes onstage, and I turn the camera to the audience, and there you are. The camera closes in. Closer and closer. Suddenly your face is filling the screen. You throw your head back, you take a deep breath . . . and you scream your lungs out!"

Debbie blinked at him for a moment. "Scream my lungs out," she repeated.

"It could be a nice touch," said Scott.

Debbie pouted. I could tell it wasn't exactly what she had in mind.

"Of course, if you'd rather not—"

Suddenly Debbie screamed!

Darwin jumped into my arms. Scott's eyes opened wide. Birds squawked and scattered from the treetops.

Debbie flashed a triumphant smile. "So . . . when do I get to meet Des?"

Chapter 5

Next morning, I awoke to a strange jungle sound.

Twaaaaangggg!

"Electric guitar?" I said. Then I remembered: Des Brodean was in the jungle. I looked out the window, and sure enough, the camp was swarming with roadies, people who travel with musicians and set up for the show. This crew had a big job to do. They were making a stage on the riverbank—from scratch!

People were coming from nearby

villages to find work and be in a video, even though I was pretty sure none of them had ever heard of Des Brodean before.

I quickly changed out of my pajamas, slathered on some sunscreen—Mom's rules—then ran outside with Darwin.

I spotted Panga in the middle of the action, talking with Scott and giving directions to the stage crew.

"Excuse me, Panga," I said, "but they're not cutting down trees in the rain forest to build this stage, are they?"

Panga smiled down at me. "Of course not, little one," he said calmly. "Everything is environmentally friendly! Trees from a tree farm, grown especially for making things. On this farm, for every tree cut down, three more are planted." He patted me on the head. "This jungle is my home. I am always taking very good care of it!"

I smiled at Panga's words. I should have

known he wouldn't do anything to harm his own home.

Suddenly there was a commotion. I glanced around. Des Brodean had emerged from his plane.

For a moment the rock star just stood there taking it all in—the jungle, Panga's camp, the busy crew hammering the stage together. It must have been the first time he'd been out of the plane since he arrived.

"I'll be right back," I told Darwin. "I have to wake up Debbie." I pushed him toward a table of doughnuts laid out for the crew.

"Take your time!" Darwin said.

I hurried into the Commvee, where Debbie was still asleep. "Des Brodean is standing right outside your window, Debbie," I told her.

At first it looked like she didn't hear. Then slowly she got up and looked out the window. She yawned. She rubbed the sleep from her eyes. Was she awake? I wasn't sure. When she reached for her pillow, I thought she was still asleep for sure.

Then I realized she just needed it to muffle a scream! There was Des Brodean in real life, not just his picture in a fan magazine. It was an awesome scream. I'm sure Scott would have been impressed. "It's HIM!" Debbie gasped hoarsely as she put her hand on her chest.

"I know." I picked up one of the fan magazines on Debbie's bed. "He looks just like himself, don't you think?"

"He's even more gorgeous," Debbie sighed.

I looked out the window to see if we were talking about the same person. Des yawned, scratched his stomach, then went back inside the plane.

"Thanks for waking me up, Eliza," Debbie said, giggling. Suddenly she began digging frantically through all her stuff.

"What is it, Debbie?" I asked. "What's wrong?"

"I'm not ready, I'm not ready!" she shrieked.

"Ready for what?"

She pulled her hair back with an elastic band, then sat cross-legged on her bed and stared into a makeup mirror she'd propped up on the window ledge. All kinds of jars, tubes, and makeup pencils lay around her on the rumpled bedspread. "I'm finally going to meet the guy of my, like, dreams! I've got work to do!"

I shook my head. I don't think I'll ever, in a million years, understand Debbie. If the "guy of her dreams" was right there, why didn't she try to talk to him? Instead of working on her face in here?

No matter. I'd done my sisterly duty. Grabbing my backpack, I headed back out to get Darwin and meet Mom and Dad, who had planned to go up the river for more filming. We were going without Debbie, who wanted to hang around the set. And this time Panga wasn't going either. He had to watch over the construction crew and be a good host to the band. Donnie was staying behind at the camp too. There were plenty of people to keep him busy!

Mom, Dad, Darwin, and I ran a boat up the river and retraced our steps into the jungle from the day before. Pretty soon we were at our old hideout, waiting.

"There's one," Dad whispered finally. Mom pointed her camera and started taping.

"Oo-oo!" Darwin said, interested.

"Shh!" Mom warned him. She had the microphone on.

Darwin's face crumpled. "Eee!" he squealed, and ran off.

"Oh, no," Mom said. "Poor Darwin. I didn't mean to hurt his feelings."

"Don't worry," I told her. "I'm sure he's okay. I'll go find him."

"Don't get lost!"

I went back the way we'd come in and found Darwin just as I emerged onto the trail. "I'm sorry, Eliza," he said. "But I just got so excited at seeing the orangutans."

"Don't worry about it, Darwin," I assured him. "I know how you feel. It was exciting to see them."

We stretched out and relaxed on a branch of the big old tree at the trailhead. The boughs were big and shady. I climbed up and leaned back against the trunk. It was so, so peaceful.

Until a nut the size of a baseball hit me on the head.

"What was that?" I said to Darwin, rubbing my head. I looked at him just in time to watch the second big nut bounce off his head—another perfect shot.

"*Who* was that?" Darwin said with a

frown, and rubbed his head.

I looked up and recognized it right away. It was my baby orangutan! "Hello again!" I said.

Then I realized the orangutan was not alone. From way up in the tree a full-size female orangutan swept down and scooped the baby into her arms. Mom to the rescue!

Dad says orangutans can walk on the ground, but most of the time they don't. Their arms are a lot longer than their legs, so it's easier for them to travel by swinging through branches rather than by walking. Away she went, with the baby hanging on like a backpack.

"Wait!" I shouted. "Don't be afraid of us! We're friendly! This is Darwin, and my name is Eliza!"

The big orangutan stopped about thirty feet up and looked over her shoulder. "You can talk?"

"It's a long story," I said.

The orangutan mother then started back down the tree in our direction. Soon we were all sharing the same branch. "My name is Kali."

"I'm Eliza, and this is Darwin," I said. "We met your baby already!"

Kali's big brown eyes looked so sad as she said, "She's not mine."

"Oh," I said, confused.

"This is Tata," she said.

That's when I noticed something about Kali—dried blood caked on her shoulder. "You're hurt!"

"Oh, Eliza, do something!" Darwin said, noticing the blood too. "Get a bandage. Some peroxide." He looked as if he were about to faint.

"My mom and dad are nearby," I told Kali. "They have medical supplies. And they'll help you."

Kali looked at me with the saddest eyes

I've ever seen. "I'm fine, really."

"But you don't look fine," I said. "Please tell me what happened."

Kali curled Tata into her arms. "Poachers," she said. "My friend An and I were looking for food two days ago. We were looking for our favorite durian tree. The fruit is delicious. It tastes like . . ." She said some words I did not understand.

"What's that mean?" I asked Darwin.

"Well, my Orangutan is not as good as my Gorilla," he said, "but I think it means 'sweet, cheesy, garlicky custard.'"

"Then"—Kali's voice broke—"some men attacked us. We fought. But there were too many of them. A loud noise rang out. I felt a pain in my arm. Then something hit me in the back of the head. . . ."

"And then what happened?" I gasped.

Kali shook her head. "When I woke up, I saw my friend lying on the ground. I shook her and called her name. But then I saw . . . she would never open her eyes again."

Tears welled up in my eyes. "Oh, no," I said softly. "I'm so sorry."

"I searched the trees," Kali went on. "At last I found my friend's baby, little Tata here. I took her into my arms and promised I would raise her as my own. But my own baby . . ." Kali's lips trembled.

I gulped, not wanting to hear.

"I . . . never found her," she said, her voice almost a whisper.

"But maybe she's still all right!" I said. "Maybe she's just lost. We'll help you find her, won't we, Darwin?"

Darwin was crying like a baby by now. "Yes, of course we will. You know how little ones are. She probably doesn't even realize—"

"It's too late," Kali pronounced gravely. "They have her. . . . I am sure of it."

I frowned at her, puzzled. "'They'?" I asked. "Who's 'they'?"

"The men," she said simply.

"But how do you know?" I asked. "Maybe—"

"It has happened before," she explained, a spark of anger in her eyes. "The men come. They kill the mothers. Then the cowards take the helpless babies."

"Where?"

Kali shook her head. "I do not know. But the babies never come home again."

A horrible pain grew in the pit of my stomach. Poachers! How could they take baby orangutans away from their mothers?

"Some say," Kali said sadly, gazing off through the trees, "that they put them in cages and take them across the waters."

"How awful!" I whispered.

"You're a lucky one," I said softly to

Tata, holding out my hand. I gasped as the baby orangutan reached out to clutch my finger. "That's it," I said, delighted. "I won't hurt you!"

Then I peered closer. "Hey, this isn't the baby orangutan we saw yesterday," I said. "Her eyes are different. They had different shades. One was light brown and the other was dark."

I looked at Kali's eyes and saw a spark of hope. "Ki had eyes like that," she said, her voice barely a whisper.

Suddenly there was a rustling in the bush. Kali gasped. Fear shined in her eyes again. Without a word, she hugged Tata close to her heart and vanished into the trees.

"We're back!" It was Mom and Dad.

"Smashing good morning," Dad said. "Excellent! I think we actually got a male orangutan on tape. And I was able to record his cry."

"That's great, Mom and Dad," I said.

I wanted to tell them about my morning too and all I had learned from Kali. But I couldn't. The shaman who gave me the power to speak to animals told me I must never tell anyone—or I'd lose my power to use it.

If I was going to rescue Kali's baby, it looked like I would have to do it on my own.

Chapter 6

"Oh, dear!" Dad said as we floated around the bend in the river in front of Panga's camp. "I think we have a bit of a parking problem."

The sun was just going down. The stage for Des Brodean's video had been completed, and now the river in front of the stage was double-parked from bank to bank with all kinds of boats—everything from dugout canoes to sleek little speed-boats. Des's band and the video crew were throwing a big party to celebrate the completion of the river stage.

"Your attention, please," someone announced from a huge stack of speakers. It was Scott.

Debbie was waiting for us at the dock. "Hurry, I think they're going to make cast announcements," she croaked.

"I want to say thank you to everyone who helped us build the stage for Des Brodean's new video," Scott announced. "It's just awesome—awesome!—and you can all be very proud!" Everyone applauded.

"As promised," Scott went on, "we're going to have a little party to celebrate this wonderful work you've completed." Everybody clapped again, louder.

"But first, I'd like to make a few announcements. Please remember that there will be a short rehearsal tomorrow afternoon for the onstage performers."

"That's what I tried out for!" Debbie exclaimed.

"What exactly did you try out for?" I asked.

"If I get the part, I'm supposed to get pulled out of the crowd by Des himself, and then we actually dance onstage, like, *together!* Then I'm supposed to totally lose it and scream! That's my close-up."

"I know you'll get the part," I whispered to Debbie. "You're a great dancer. And nobody can top your scream."

Then Des stepped up to the microphone, along with an acoustic guitar.

"Oh, wow," Debbie said, looking faint. "He's unplugged."

"I'd like to play a little something I wrote for everybody who helped us with the stage," Des said.

A hush fell over the crowd as he began to strum softly. He sang:

"This is for everyone
Who helped with the stage.

This is for everyone
Who helped with the stage.
This is for everyone
Who helped with the stage.
Thanks a lot . . .
For helping with the stage."

"Ohhh! Totally awesome," Debbie sighed when it was over.

"Hey, they didn't announce the parts," I told Debbie.

"No, they didn't," she said, looking disappointed.

"Come on, Darwin," I said. "Let's get something to eat." I looked around. "Where is he?"

Debbie shrugged. She was in a daze.

"I have to find Darwin," I told her. "Don't worry, you'll get the part. I'll catch up with you later."

I walked in the direction of the Commvee, searching the crowd as I went.

We'd been getting up pretty early on this trip. And we'd spent the last two days on the river and in the jungle. Maybe Darwin went to bed early for a change, even though it didn't seem like him to go to bed without saying good night.

I opened the door to the Commvee and peered inside. "Darwin?" I called softly.

There was no answer, so I went in to check. His hammock was empty.

Standing in the doorway, I looked out into the night. Where could Darwin be?

Suddenly I heard a noise—*PSST!*—and I nearly jumped right out of my skin! Was it a snake? Was it poisonous?

"Eliza!"

It knew my name! Then I realized it was a voice I'd know anywhere. I saw something move in the bush, then walked over to it. "Darwin!" I started to say. "What are you do—"

"Shh! The camp is surrounded by

orangutans," he told me. "I've been listening to them in the trees."

I tried to see, but the trees were too thick. "What are they doing around the camp?"

Darwin shrugged. "How should I know? They're orangutans, I'm a chimpanzee. We're not that close."

"You're both apes," I said, then added, "I meant that in a nice way, of course."

I glanced up at the camp office. The light was on inside. "Come on, Darwin," I said. "Maybe Panga will know something."

Through the screen door of his office, I saw Panga sitting at his desk. He was on the phone. "Mr. Brodean doesn't know it, but he will be carrying some extra luggage," I heard him say. "Yes, two bags. Be sure and tell the gas man."

What was Panga talking about? I moved closer to the doorway. Darwin whined, "Let's go!"

"Shh!" I said.

And Panga heard me. Stepping outside, he demanded, "Who's there?"

I had to think fast. "Oh! Hi, there!" I said, standing up. "It's me, Eliza Thornberry! I was just looking for my chimp!" I picked Darwin up in my arms like a baby.

"Ah," Panga answered, nodding. "Sometimes apes can be very difficult to handle."

"Yeah, they can be kind of mischievous," I agreed. "Well, I'll just take him home now. Thanks for leaving a light on!"

"Yes. Time to run along now," Panga said sternly. He watched as I carried Darwin down the hill.

"I don't know if I like being called 'mischievous,'" Darwin said as we came to the Commvee. "Spider monkeys are mischievous. We chimps are much more civilized."

"Kali, Kali," I called out softly, hoping that she was there and would come down and talk.

But they were gone—either scared away by the noise and lights . . . or by poachers? I thought about what had happened to Kali. And then I thought about Panga. Did he know what was happening with the orangutans? What did he mean when he said that Des Brodean was going to be carrying extra luggage?

I kept thinking about Ki. And Tata's dead mother. And I knew I had to find out.

Chapter 7

"Des is having what?" Debbie screeched the next morning when I tried to wake her up.

"Having breakfast with us at the Commvee," I told her. "He and Dad hit it off really well at the party last night. Didn't you see?"

Debbie thumped her pillow. "No! I kept trying to meet Des all night. But I could never find him in the crowd."

"Did you know Des is a big fan of the show?"

Debbie frowned. "What show?"

"Dad's show! And guess what! Dad used to be in a band!"

"Oh, no," Debbie moaned. "Was that back when he still had that little ponytail?"

"I think it was during college," I said.

Debbie tumbled out of bed and stared at her mirror. "I need to wash my hair!"

"Before you can have breakfast?"

"Before I can have breakfast with Des Brodean!" she exclaimed. She grabbed a bottle of something. "Maybe if I just sort of spritz it . . ."

"See you in a few minutes," I said, heading outside. When I opened the door, there was Des Brodean.

"Hi," said the famous rock star, just like a normal person. "I'm Des, and your dad . . ."

"My dad invited you to breakfast," I said. For a rock-and-roll star, Mr. Brodean seemed kind of shy. "I'm Eliza, and I'm sure Dad will be here soon."

"Cool . . ."

It was my first time talking to a rock star, but he seemed like a regular guy. I walked him over to the picnic table. He seemed a lot calmer in person, not mad at everything like he seemed onstage and in the magazines. I was impressed, actually. I mean, he's probably eaten in all kinds of fancy restaurants with celebrities and royalty. But he sat down at our picnic table like it was the best table in town.

My sister, Debbie, on the other hand, was acting like somebody from another planet.

I heard the door to the Commvee creak and I looked over. Debbie didn't come out, but I knew she was there, peeking through the crack. I also heard a little muffled *eek!* Des didn't seem to notice; he probably thought it was the sound of an animal in the jungle.

"Hey, Debbie," I called, and pulled on the door.

"Eliza!" she hissed, holding the doorknob on the other side.

I yanked back. "Why don't you come . . ."

Ugh! I pulled so hard, I fell backward onto the ground, and Debbie flew out, tumbling down on top of me.

"I was coming, already!" she muttered, then scrambled to her feet. Words spilled out of her mouth at Des Brodean. "I love the way your guitar catches on fire at the end of 'You Burn Me Up.' That is, like, my all-time favorite song!"

Des smiled politely. "It's my mom's favorite too."

"And the way you fall off the stage in the music video for the song 'I Feel Down'? I bet you didn't even use a stuntman for that!" she said.

He blushed.

Just then Dad came dashing into the

campsite. "Oh, hello, everyone!" He chuckled and held up a coffee can full of small black berries. "Found some treats to go with the pancakes!"

The meal went pretty well. Des was very polite. He didn't bat an eye when Donnie drank from the syrup bottle. And he hardly noticed when Darwin picked a bug out of his hair—and ate it.

I guess a famous rock star like Des Brodean has seen it all.

We shot until noon, then took a lunch break in the shade of the Commvee.

"Mom," I said, "what's going to be in the show about orangutans being an endangered species?"

"You mean, about what's causing the problem?" she replied.

I nodded.

"Well, the biggest reason seems to be timber farming—cutting down trees. I'm sure we'll say something about that."

"What about poaching?" I said.

"Yes, poaching's a big problem too," she said.

"I heard they steal the babies," I said.

Before she could answer, a voice behind me said, "Ah, there you are!" It was Panga. "Nigel has been looking all over for you!"

We followed him to the river stage, where Des, Scott, and my dad were talking about the concert.

"There you are, my dear," Dad said when he saw Mom. "Mr. Free has informed me that Deborah has a part in the show. And he has a smashing idea about taping the whole thing, and I wanted to see what you think. You too, Eliza."

Scott pointed up and we all looked. High in a tree above our heads was a tiny platform. "Okay," he said, "because the concert is to promote orangutan awareness, I am thinking—dig this—we shoot the concert from the trees. Get it? To show the orangutan's point of view. What do you guys think? Awesome or what?"

"And we could use the footage for our show," Dad said. "Really give the viewer a taste of what it's like to be an orangutan, looking down on the human population!"

Mom nodded. "I like it," she said.

Dad looked at me. "What do you think, Eliza?"

"Great!" I said.

"Wonderful!" Scott said to my mom. "How about this, Marianne? I'll shoot from up close to the stage. You will shoot from the treetops!"

"You must be joking!" she said, laughing. "Me? Up there?"

"It's quite safe, Marianne," Dad assured her. "I personally inspected the seat when Mr. Free first brought up the idea."

Suddenly we heard a wild scream from the audience. The crowd roared. The Des Brodean show was about to begin.

Chapter 8

Pressing the TALK button on the walkie-talkie, I looked up at the tree that towered over the stage.

"You okay up there, Mom?" I said.

The walkie-talkie made a crackling noise, then she answered, "I'm okay! Tie your shoelace!"

I chuckled. Mom was fifty feet up a tree, peering down at me through the zoom lens on her video camera.

Des Brodean's band—a drummer and a bass guitar player—were already onstage, tuning up for the show. A crowd of Sumatrans was standing by to watch. Boats rocked on the river. All that was missing was Des Brodean himself. But not for long.

Suddenly the stage rumbled deeply. Was it an earthquake? But then the crowd cheered and trapdoors opened in front of the band. A blue fog rolled out of the openings, and big beams of white light switched on. In the mist they looked like white tree trunks growing out of the stage.

Then I heard a giant hissing noise and watched a black, mountainous shape rise steadily from center stage.

"Why, I've never seen anything like it!" Darwin exclaimed. "An inflatable volcano!"

There on the top was Des, riding it as calmly as you would an elevator. It really was kind of amazing.

All of a sudden there was a loud *POP!* and the whole place went pitch-black! For a couple of stunned seconds, it was totally quiet.

After staring at the bright lights, I couldn't see anything. But then I heard someone say something, and then someone else say something, and before long everybody was talking at once. The only other noise was the hiss of the volcano deflating.

"I believe they've blown a fuse," Darwin said.

I wasn't surprised. Panga's camp didn't have power from an electric company. It was all from generators, which were probably overloaded by the band's special effects.

"There ought to be something we can do," I said as I pulled out the flashlight I was still carrying from my river trip.

"Well, that's handy," Darwin said.

"Come on." I ducked under the stage and followed the cables out the other side. They snaked along the grass all the way up to a little toolshed-size building in back of Panga's office.

"That's the generator house, where the power's made," Darwin said. "The fuses will be inside."

"We're in luck," I said, shining the flashlight at the front of the building. "Someone's left the door open." Then I shined the light on the latch and gasped.

The lock was broken.

"Someone *forced* the door open," Darwin said nervously.

I snapped the flashlight off and we froze, wondering if anyone was still inside.

"Ah-hah!" someone cried.

Someone stumbled up behind us in the dark.

Chapter 7

It was Panga. He'd arrived along with a helper carrying a toolbox. "Eliza Thornberry!" he said. "What are you doing here? Very dangerous!"

"Uh, I was just about to see if there was anything we, uh, I mean, I, could do," I told him. "You know . . . " I flicked the flashlight on and wiggled the beam over the generator house behind him.

I stopped myself from gasping just in time.

I'd seen an apelike figure in the beam of

the flashlight, and a faint tuft of red hair. An orangutan was behind the generator house! Panga turned to look, but it ducked away. I wondered if the ape had anything to do with the power going out. . . .

Suddenly it was back on.

I turned around and looked down the hill at the stage. The crowd cheered. The inflatable volcano was rising again. Then the band started up too.

Panga turned to face me. Grabbing my shoulders, he warned, "You must not come here again. It's not safe for a girl like you!"

"Have a good time now!" he added, steering us back toward the concert. I had the feeling he was really steering us away from something else that was around that generator house. But what?

Onstage Des stepped up to make an announcement to the crowd, which was going wild from the first song. Scott was there too, getting it all on videotape.

"This next song is dedicated to our very good buddies—the Sumatran orangutans!" he shouted. He stared into the camera, and a huge close-up shot stared out at us from the big video screen onstage. "Hey, hairy red dudes—we know you're out there, okay? Let's hear it for the orangutans!"

The crowd roared.

"We know you're endangered, but you can forget about becoming extinct, know what I mean? 'Cause we're there for you! This song is for the orangutan!"

BWAANNG! Des strummed his guitar.

Again the crowd roared and the band cranked out the music and Des sang.

"This is a song for the orangutan!
Don't cut down his tree!
I'm talking to you,

Now listen to me!
He lives in that tree!
Happy and free!
That's how it's gonna be! YEAH!"

For a second I wondered if all the noise might be bad for the wildlife. Then I remembered that Sumatra's mountain range is actually a bunch of active volcanoes. Des Brodean's band could have been just another eruption.

After a half hour the band was ready to take a break. Des told the crowd they'd be back. "But, meanwhile, I'd like to take this opportunity to say thank you to our host, Mr. Panga Boute, who made this event possible," he said.

Everybody looked around, expecting Panga to stand and take a bow. But he wasn't around.

"Well, let's give him a big hand wherever he is!" Des Brodean said, and there was a polite round of applause.

"I think I know where he is," I whispered to Darwin. "Around that generator house! Come on!"

"Y-You mean g-go there?" Darwin stuttered. "It's dark!"

"Don't worry," I told him. "I've got a flashlight, remember?"

All the way up I kept the flashlight beam small and close to my feet until we were near the shed, then I turned it off. Slowly our eyes adjusted to the darkness.

"There he is," I whispered.

It was Panga, all right. He was using a hand truck to cart a box from the generator shed over to Des Brodean's plane.

"Bet you he goes back for another one," I said. Sure enough, out of the shed came box number two.

"Those are cages, Darwin," I whispered. "Disguised as musical instrument cases.

Panga's been kidnapping orangutans . . . he's a poacher."

Darwin shuddered. "You're sure they're not just ordinary, everyday, old musical instruments?"

"Remember what Panga said on the phone?" I said. "When he talked about extra luggage on Des Brodean's plane, he meant orangutans. He said to tell the gas man—that's their contact at the airport. When the plane stops for fuel, they'll unload the crates and turn them over to the bad guys."

"Great," Darwin said. "Let's go notify the authorities."

I shook my head. "You're forgetting something. In this part of Sumatra, Panga *is* the authorities."

"Then let's tell your mom and dad."

"Except the evidence is on Des Brodean's plane. Panga will say Des is the guilty one, smuggling them out as pets. No, we have to help them escape. That's where you come in."

Darwin gave me a worried look.

"Those animals were probably already very suspicious of humans before they were caught," I told him. "I don't even want to think about what they might do if another human opened their cages."

Darwin nodded. "I suppose you're right," he admitted. "But Panga will get away and smuggle again."

"Maybe," I said. "But you know what Panga himself told me—the jungle takes care of itself. I have the strangest feeling those words are going to come back to haunt him."

Chapter 10

I never found out how Panga got to be the number one bully in his corner of Sumatra. But I figured out how he stayed there—by not taking any chances!

He'd put one man on guard duty by the plane. A very big man.

"Don't worry, Darwin," I said. "There are two of us, and only one of him. That means the odds are two to one in our favor."

"He's bigger than four of us," Darwin whined. With squinted, watery eyes and bared teeth, he looked ready to cry any minute.

"What a face you have, Darwin," I said. "And you've just given me a great idea!" I stuck my flashlight under his chin and switched it on. With the light shining up at his miserable grimace, Darwin looked positively hideous.

"What?" he said.

"Remember that story Panga told?" I reminded him. "About Rabi?"

"The spirit who lives in the forest," Darwin whispered.

"The one who turns people into trees," I said. "Everybody here believes it, and they're terrified of him."

"So?" asked Darwin, frowning.

I shook out my hair, grimaced, and stuck the flashlight under my chin. "Meet Rabi," I said.

The expression on Darwin's face told me I was getting the look I wanted. "You look positively frightful!"

"Thank you," I said. "Now, let's go turn somebody into a tree."

Together Darwin and I circled around the big building, then crept to the generator house. "You'll have to work fast," I warned Darwin. "Just get to the plane, and I'll join you as quickly as I can." Then I walked into the open.

As soon as I stepped out from behind the safety of the generator house, the guard seemed to grow ten feet taller. If I could scare him half as much as he was already scaring me, I knew I would be all right. I crept behind a tree, peeked out from behind it, then shined the flashlight on my horrible hairy face. "Ahhh-ooo . . . ," I whined softly.

The guard turned around just as I turned off the flashlight.

I sneaked over to another tree and did the same thing. This time I whispered loudly, "Rabi wants you, Rabi wants you. . . ." Just before I turned off the flashlight, I saw that the guard's eyes had opened wide. He was getting scared!

Slipping to a tree closer to the guard, I repeated my scary performance, this time adding more sound effects. "Ah-ooo, ah-ooo, Rabi is coming for you . . . chuh-chuh-chuh-chuh . . . Rabi is coming for you . . . NOW!"

Then I swayed side to side and moved closer to him. "Rabi is coming NOW," I shouted. "Now, now, now, now, now!"

I was five steps away from him when I decided to give him the total Rabi effect. "AIEEEEE!" I screamed. "Rabi will turn you into a TREE!"

You've probably seen someone do the hundred-yard dash. But have you seen them do it backward? It's quite a sight.

Even the sound of the concert couldn't totally drown out his frightened cries as he disappeared into the night screaming, "Rabi! Rabi!"

"It worked, Darwin!" I yelled. He was already at the plane, yanking open the cargo door. I ran to his side.

"Make sure they see you first," I told him as we dragged the heavy trunk-cages out of the hold. We flipped the latches and opened the lids, and—presto! There they were!

"She's with me," Darwin told the frightened young orangutans. "And you're free to go." You never saw babies move so fast. In a flash they scrambled up the nearest tree. Just in time to see Panga return with the angriest look on his face you ever saw.

"What are you doing?!" he screamed.

I thought it was pretty obvious.

By this point there were about thirty full-grown orangutans in the surrounding trees that knew we were on their side. So when they saw Panga and his guard coming for us, they came down to help out.

Instantly Panga and his friend put on the brakes. Against me and Darwin he might have had a chance. But against a couple dozen angry apes? The two men wheeled around and took off in the opposite direction—straight for the concert.

"Don't let them get away!" I yelled. Darwin and the orangutans and I took off after them like a posse.

Debbie was just stepping onto the stage to dance with Des when Panga and his guard and Darwin and I and the angry mob of orangutans came down the hill and streamed into the crowd. It was pandemonium. Panga was screaming, the orangutans were screaming, the crowd was screaming . . .

And Debbie was screaming, her voice

blasting from the band's speakers at ten times the usual volume.

It was a wonder I heard the walkie-talkie in my back pocket squawk. I remembered Mom, high up in the tree.

"Come in, Mom!" I said. "Are you okay?"

"I'm fine, honey, are you all right?" she answered. "What was that all about?"

"It's a really long story," I told her. "Did you get it on video?"

"Well, I taped Panga and somebody being chased by orangutans," she said. "But I don't know what it was all about."

"It's sort of complicated," I said into the walkie-talkie, "but Panga's a poacher. He was going to smuggle baby orangutans out of the country on Des Brodean's plane, but Darwin and I let them out. Over!" I took my finger off the TALK button and waited.

After a moment she replied, "You miss a lot when you're stuck up a tree, you know?"

Chapter 11

Darwin and I sat quietly, waiting for the sound of leaves rustling overhead.

"Here they come," he said at last.

In the morning light we saw them. Two orangutans swinging gracefully through the upper stories.

"Kali!" I shouted.

They stopped. Kali and her baby, Ki—they were back together. Kali called out, "Come on, Tata," and another baby orangutan emerged through the thick leaves.

We laughed as Tata playfully climbed

onto Ki's back. Ki started hopping up and down, gently batting at Tata.

Darwin and I waved at the orangutans, and they waved back. Then they continued on, into the jungle that was their home.

"I'll miss them," Darwin said.

"Me too," I replied. "But that will be a nice way to remember them—disappearing into the trees."

Chapter 12

"Hello, Mr. Boute's office. May I help you?"
I said, answering Panga's phone. "No, Mr.
Boute is tied up right now. . . ."

Panga glared at me across the room.
He strained against the ropes that held
him to his own desk chair.

"If you'll leave me your number, I'll
have Mr. Boute call you as soon as he's
available," I added.

I knew now that Panga's AOS organiza-
tion was a fake. It was just a cover for
smugglers.

Fortunately for us, it would be years before Panga would be able to return the call. Indonesian government officials were on their way, and I couldn't wait to show them the cages in the generator shed and Mom's tape of angry orangutans chasing Panga.

"As soon as the Sumatran police arrive, I want you girls to go straight to the Commvee," Mom said. "We have a tight schedule to keep."

"Another jungle?" I asked hopefully. "The Gobi Desert? Mount Everest? That's not too far. . . ."

Debbie groaned. "Stop! Please . . . don't tell me where we're going," she pleaded. "I'd rather not know."

"Nonsense, Deborah!" Dad said. "After all, you're wearing the map! We're headed about an inch over from your left shoulder."

Debbie looked down at her Des Brodean Unsanitary Tour T-shirt. "Hong

Kong?" she said. "Dad, that is so awesome!"

"Yes, quite!" Dad said. "We're producing a show at the Hong Kong Zoological and Botanical Garden. All about legal protection for animals, encouraging zoos to report suspicious animal dealers who try to sell them endangered creatures. Helping the zoos inform the visiting public to beware of them as well. With their help, you know, it will be the *poacher* who will be in danger of becoming extinct."

Debbie let out a happy sigh. But it wasn't about the show. "Another Des Brodean concert," she murmured contentedly.

Another Des Brodean concert. Oh, well. It wasn't a jungle, or a desert, or the top of a mountain.

But at least it would be *wild*.

Discovery Facts

Banyan: A banyan tree is easy to identify, with roots growing down from its branches to form new tree trunks. Banyan trees are about one hundred feet tall and can live for more than one hundred years.

Durian: Called "the king of fruits" in Southeast Asia, this football-shaped fruit has a hard, thorny shell. It also has a distinctive pungent smell, and the edible part of the fruit, found in compartments inside the shell, is sweet and custardlike.

Hornbill: A type of bird that lives in Africa and Southeast Asia and is famous for its big, banana-shaped bill. This bill comes in handy when the female hornbill is nesting deep within rock walls or tree trunks. The male hornbill passes food to her on the end of his long bill!

Orangutan: In the language of the native Malay people, *orang hutan* means "man of the forest." With their long arms, orangutans spend most of their life swinging in the branches of the trees, almost never touching the ground!

Sumatra: Forty million people live on this large island that is part of the country of Indonesia. A chain of volcanoes rises over Sumatra's western coastline, and eruptions happen all the time!

About the Authors

Cathy East Dubowski and **Mark Dubowski** started writing and illustrating children's books while they lived in a small apartment in New York City. Now they live and work in Chapel Hill, North Carolina, and have written several books featuring the Rugrats and The Wild Thornberrys. Just like Nigel and Marianne, they have two daughters, Megan and Lauren, who are about the same age as Eliza and Debbie. The Dubowski family also shares the Thornberrys' love for animals, and has two dogs, two hamsters, and a guinea pig.